Bear at Ho
L'Ours à la maison

Stella Blackstone
Debbie Harter

This is Bear's house, and this is the key.

Voici la maison de l'Ours, et voici la clé.

Open the door,
and what do you see?

Ouvre la porte :
qu'est-ce que tu vois ?

This is the kitchen, all clean and neat,

Voici la cuisine,
bien propre et nette,

And this is the dining room, where Bear likes to eat.

**Et voici la salle à manger,
où l'Ours aime manger.**

**This is the playroom,
with a big toy chest,**

Voici la salle de jeux, avec un grand coffre à jouets,

And this is the living room, where Bear likes to rest.

Et voici le salon,
où l'Ours aime se reposer.

**This is the hallway,
where Bear climbs the stairs,**

Voici l'entrée,
d'où l'Ours monte l'escalier,

And this is the study, with a big armchair.

**Et voici le bureau,
avec un gros fauteuil.**

**This is the bathroom,
with walls painted bright,**

Voici la salle de bains,
aux murs de couleurs vives,

And this is the bedroom, where Bear says goodnight!

Et voici la chambre,
où l'Ours dit « Bonne nuit ! »

Downstairs
En bas

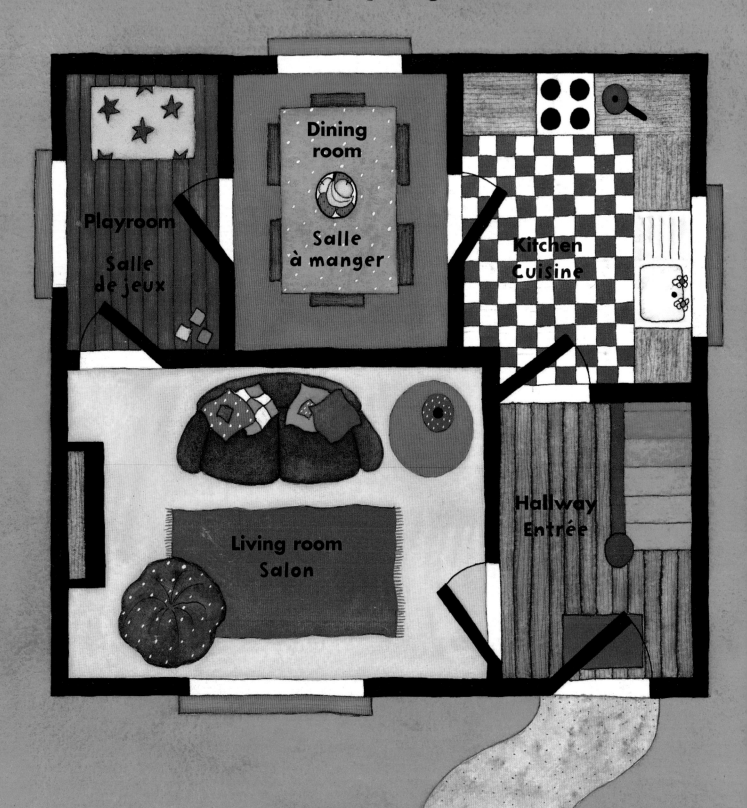

Playroom

Salle
de jeux

Dining
room

Salle
à manger

Kitchen
Cuisine

Living room
Salon

Hallway
Entrée

Upstairs
En haut

Bathroom
Salle de bains

Study
Bureau

Bedroom
Chambre

Stairs
Escalier

Landing
Palier

Vocabulary / Vocabulaire

tree – l'arbre

flower – la fleur

oven – le four

table – la table

cat – le chat

sofa – le canapé

mirror – le miroir

book – le livre

bath – la baignoire

bed – le lit

Barefoot Books
124 Walcot Street
Bath, BA1 5BG, UK

Barefoot Books
2067 Massachusetts Ave
Cambridge, MA 02140, USA

Text copyright © 2001 by Stella Blackstone Illustrations copyright © 2001 by Debbie Harter
Translated by Servane Champion

The moral rights of Stella Blackstone and Debbie Harter have been asserted

First published in Great Britain by Barefoot Books Ltd in 2001 and in the United States of America
by Barefoot Books Inc in 2001. This edition published in 2010

This book has been printed in China by Hung Hing Off-set Printing Ltd on 100% acid-free paper

ISBN 978-1-84686-421-6

1 3 5 7 9 8 6 4 2

British Cataloguing-in-Publication Data:
a catalogue record for this book is available from the British Library

Library of Congress Cataloging-in-Publication Data is available upon request